LOCK HOLMES

PHILIP MARLOWE

BRENDAN
O'GOOLEY

MS
BIRKINSTEAD

THE BEARD BROTHERS

SHARA

GIZMO

DALE

MRS MATRINGHAM

MRS CROMPTON

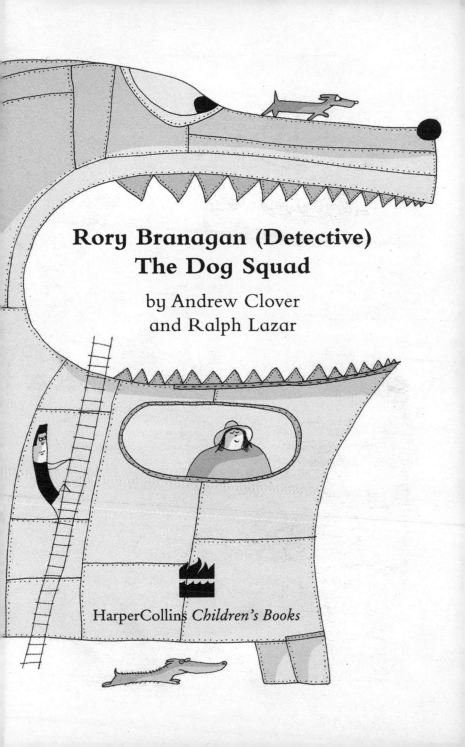

Rory Branagan (Detective)
The Dog Squad

by Andrew Clover
and Ralph Lazar

HarperCollins *Children's Books*

First published in Great Britain by HarperCollins *Children's Books* in 2018
HarperCollins *Children's Books* is a division of HarperCollins*Publishers* Ltd,
HarperCollins Publishers, 1 London Bridge Street, London SE1 9GF

The HarperCollins website address is:
www.harpercollins.co.uk

1

ISBN 978-0-00-826586-1

Andrew Clover and Ralph Lazar assert their moral rights to be identified as
the author and illustrator of the work.

Typeset in Palatino Roman 14/22 pt
Printed and bound in England by CPI Group (UK) Ltd,
Croydon CR0 4YY

MIX
Paper from
responsible sources
FSC C007454
FSC
www.fsc.org
™

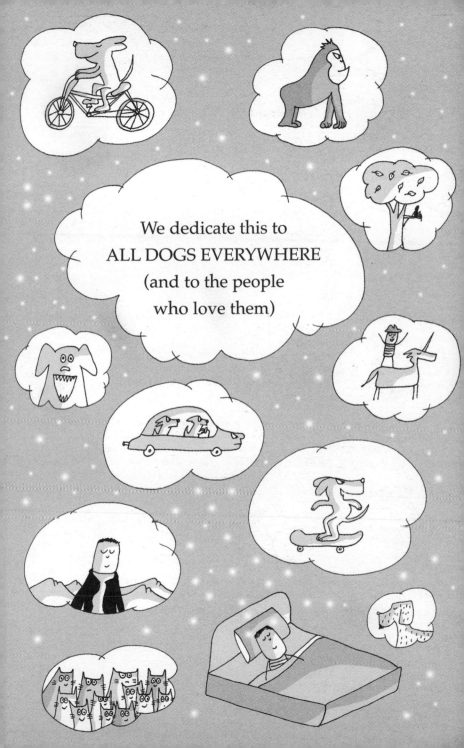

We dedicate this to
ALL DOGS EVERYWHERE
(and to the people
who love them)

I am Rory Branagan.

I am actually a detective.

Only three days ago, I, with my new

Best Friend and Accomplice, Cassidy

'the Cat' Callaghan, trailed some

poisoners to the Deadly Pirate

restaurant, where we *GOT*

THEM!!

Soon I am going to be the *Biggest*

Detective in the World!!

I am even going to solve the *biggest mystery in my life*, which is: WHERE IS MY DAD?

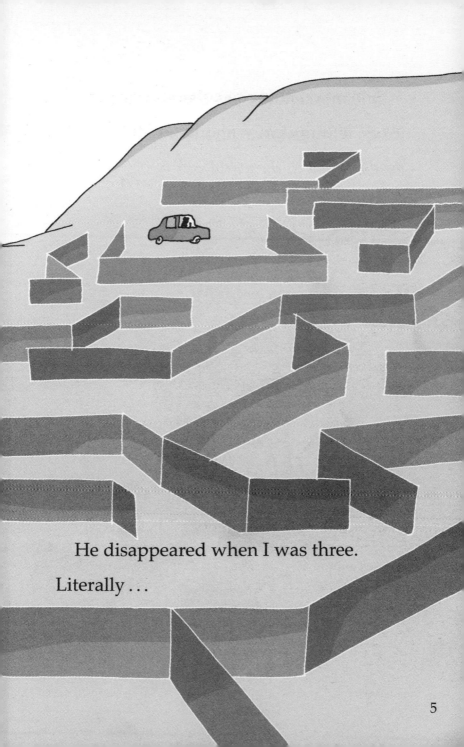

He disappeared when I was three.

Literally . . .

One moment he was there – cracking jokes, telling stories and being the *deadliest dad in the world.*

And the next, he was gone.

BUT THEN ...

Three days ago, I got a *secret letter* from him. He said he was hiding *in the place where he was once happiest*. So now I know he's *alive*, but I'm thinking ...

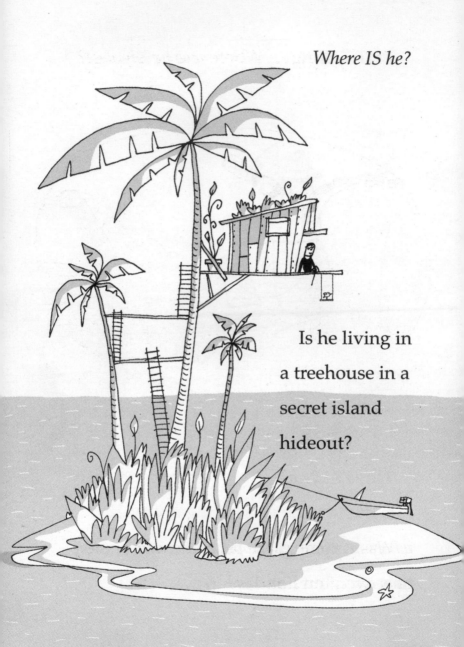

Where IS he?

Is he living in a treehouse in a secret island hideout?

I'm thinking ... Where *was he happiest?*

Was it some place far away, where he
once went on holiday?

I ask my brother who is *looming*
by the hallway mirror. He got the first
four hairs of his moustache last week,
and now he rushes out, ten times a day, to
see if more have appeared.

'Where do you think Dad is?' I ask.

'I don't know,' he says. 'I *do* know Mum
gets cross if we even ask.'

'OK,' I say, 'where do you think he was happiest?'

'Why are you even *asking*?' he says.

'Because,' I tell him, 'I am just ... being a detective.'

'MUM!!!'

he shouts.

'He's BEING A DETECTIVE AGAIN!'

And, two seconds later, Mum appears,

and already she looks set to *blow up*.

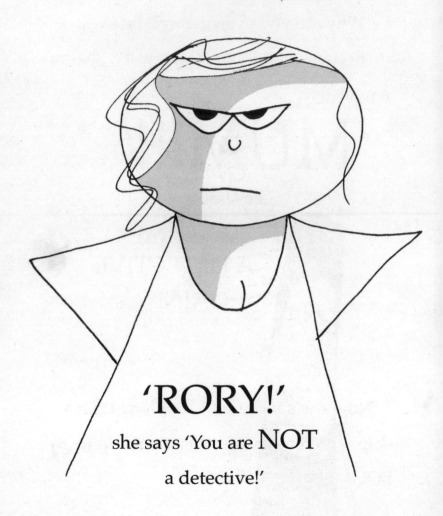

'RORY!'

she says 'You are NOT

a detective!'

'I *am*,' I reply. 'Even the policeman said so when I solved a *crime*.'

Now she's more set to explode than a ship with ten *cannons* that are about to go BOOM.

'Rory,' she says, 'you need to think about OTHER PEOPLE. I am *trying* to keep this family together, and it's *hard enough* without you getting into danger. There are some *bad people* out there. Last time you were being a detective you hurt your leg *very badly*.'

Now THAT is a *tiny bit true*, I suppose.

I did sprain my leg very badly, which is why I am supposed to be spending ONE WHOLE WEEK in bed wearing a surgical boot.

'But I did not hurt my leg because of *bad people*,' I say, 'but because I jumped over a high gate, and landed next to a pig . . .'

And that *does* it. Suddenly my mum . . .

...BLOWS UP like a ship with a *hundred cannons* that are all *BLASTING OFF*.

'NO!!!

I do *not* want some story!' she screams.

'I just need you to stay in your bed doing your homework, and, if I find you've been being a detective, you will be in the **worst trouble** of your life!'

But even as Mum is shouting I am
thinking: *But I LOVE being a detective!*
I am thinking: *I even like getting into danger!*
And I swear . . . it is literally only
about an hour after that . . .

... that Cat and I discover a *real, actual crime*, and end up getting into the very *DEADLIEST OF DEADLY DANGERS*!!! I'll tell you the whole story.

CHAPTER ONE:
A Call to Adventure

It all starts ... with me doing something that is not DANGEROUS at all. I am lying in my room. I am having a cool, *relaxing* time reading a book.

It is about Napoleon.

Apparently he was only small but he
became the most *powerful person in the
world,* and I am thinking ... *I am only
small. I could become the most powerful
person in the world.*

Suddenly my brother's **big head** appears.

'There is someone at the door for you,' he says.

'Who is it?' I ask.

But he just goes.

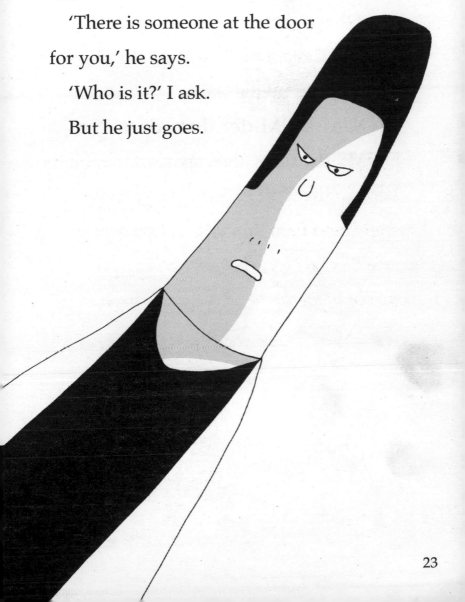

But I don't mind.

You don't need to be a genius to *detect* that the person coming is Cassidy 'the Cat' Callaghan. I can hear her *singing* as she comes up the stairs.

'DUM-DUM-der-dum-dum-DUM!' she sings, then she ...

leaps into the room.

'Hello, *Deadly*!' she says. (That's what she calls me!)

'Hello, Cat!' I reply. (That's what I call her!)

'So,' she says, 'will we go out to trace clues and solve crimes?'

'Er ... no,' I say. 'I can't just now ...
because of my leg!'

'Oh, I won't let you be stopped by
a little thing like that! I have prepared
something!' she says. 'Come on! I'll give
you a piggyback.'

I get on her back and she piggybacks
me out of the room and down the stairs.

'Behold,' she says. 'Your *chariot*!'

It's a bin.

'I am NOT going in there!' I tell her.

'I have *cleaned* it,' she says, 'and I've put in cushions, and I also have something *very detectivey* to show you!'

So now she's got me *interested*.

'Stand back!' I command. 'I shall *mount the chariot*!'

I get in and she rolls me out the door.

'*Charge!*' she shouts, and she starts to *sprint* up the street.

As
we go I
am looking
at the
weirdest dog.
He's tied to a
lamppost. He's got
short legs, but he's
got the longest back
you ever saw; he looks
like a furry crocodile. But I
love all dogs.

'Hello,
boy!'
I call.

He wags
his tail, and
you can see he's
friendly. So now
I'm longing to go
back and stroke him.
But the Cat is in the
mood to go fast.

'*Full speed!*' she says.

She *hurtles* all the way to the shop where the *detectivey thing* she wants to show me turns out to be a magazine called *Real Detective*, but we haven't actually brought *money* to buy it, and also I can't go in the shop in my bin.

So we read by the door. I see right away that *Real Detective* is *brilliant*. We open it and we find 'Secrets of the Famous Detectives' . . .

REAL DETECTIVE

SECRETS OF
THE FAMOUS DETECTIVES

SHERLOCK HOLMES:

Secret: Notice

EVERYTHING.

We turn over the page. There's ...

REAL DETECTIVE

SECRETS OF
THE FAMOUS DETECTIVES

№ 2

HERCULE POIROT
Secret: List all
suspects. List
their motives.

№ 3

PHILIP MARLOWE
Secret: Don't be
afraid to *fight*.

I am just thinking that I LOVE this magazine when I ... Rory Branagan (detective) NOTICE a real, actual crime.

A clue hits me in the face. It's a piece of paper blown by the wind.

It says ...

'Lost: Ben, our much-loved greyhound dog.'

And there's a picture of a dog looking sad.

I then notice on a lamppost ...

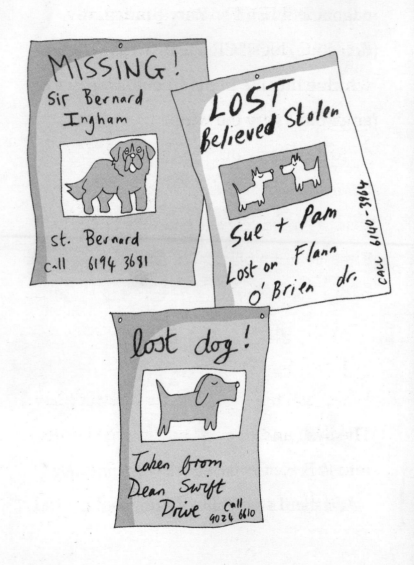

Right away my heart is beating. I cannot BELIEVE someone is actually TAKING dogs from Dean Swift Drive, which is my *actual road*. I am already very angry, but very curious.

'Rory,' says Cat, 'look.'

I look, and at the other end of the road *someone is taking the furry crocodile*. They've got a black coat and a black wool hat.

'Is that dog . . .?' I start.

'Being stolen?' says Cat.

You can tell the crocodile doesn't like it. The thief and dog are turning the corner into Roy Keane Close.

'*Quick!*' I say. 'Follow that dog!'

It's two hundred metres but Cat RUNS
all the way.

But when we get to Roy Keane Close,
there's NO ONE there.

We run down it.

We look left. There's NO ONE.

We look right. There's NO ONE.

We look in the trees. There's NO ONE.

We turn round.

There's Corner Boy, my neighbour.

He's standing on his corner, but he's
staring up at a window on Jay Byrne
Road.

'Corner Boy!' I shout. 'Did you just see
a person stealing a dog?'

'No! All I saw was that Jack Russell up there,' he says (pointing up to the left). 'He always goes WILD if anyone goes past.'

'Did he go wild?'

'No.'

Cat turns to me. 'So,' she says, 'that means the thief did not go up there.'

'Could they be hiding in one of those cars?' I say.

'Good thinking!' says Cat.

She sprints past all the cars. She looks into all of them, then runs back.

'I saw nothing,' she pants. 'That means whoever took that dog MUST have gone into one of these five houses!'

I'm thinking: *She could be right!* But I'm also thinking: *But, if she's wrong, then the dog thief could still be OUT and ABOUT and if they are, they MIGHT TAKE WILKINS WELKIN!!!!!*

But some people might not know who Wilkins Welkin is.

I shall explain . . .

CHAPTER TWO:
Wilkins Welkin, King of Dogs

When my mum goes out she always invites over Mrs Welkin, the old lady from across the road, and before she leaves she ALWAYS says, 'Are you *sure* you'll be OK?'

It's AS IF Mum thinks that as soon as she goes out Mrs Welkin is *leaping over the wall with a sword* . . .

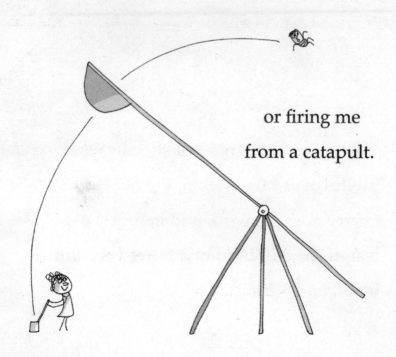

or firing me from a catapult.

I actually *love* it when Mrs Welkin comes, because she brings Wilkins Welkin, her sausage dog.

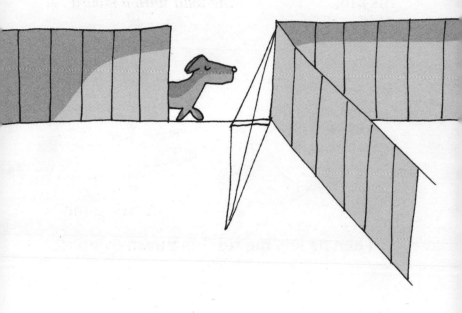

You wouldn't know it to see him, but he is *quite a character*.

As soon as he sees me
he goes *BERSERK* –
leaping about
and *wagging*
his tail.

Then he lets me rub his tummy.

Then, suddenly, he *starts his tricks*.

First he does two or three commando rolls.

Then he sprints into the living room, then

he LEAPS UP to the windowsill where ...

... he starts madly yanking on the

blind, going *rrr-rrr-rrrr*.

(I have no idea why he does that!)

But then suddenly
he leaps off again.

He powers up the stairs ...

He pokes open my
door with his nose ...

He leaps on my bed ...

... and he gets *straight down to business* staring out of the window.

He stares out for ages.

It's as if he knows that, if he turns his attention away *for a moment* . . .

... in that moment *twenty cats will go by.*

They'll be swinging on the washing line.

They'll be entering the house.

In no time at all they will be *romping* around everywhere, *scratching* and leaving *fur* and their evil catty *stink*.

Wilkins is determined that this will NOT happen. (Not on his watch.) He looks out *for ages*.

I *love* it when he does that. I *love* Wilkins Welkin. And to my horror I realise that, as we went running past down the street just now, I saw *him in his garden*.

'Quick!' I shout. 'Take me back to Mrs Welkin's!'

Cat dashes down past Corner Boy.
We *shoot* down the middle of the street
towards Mrs Welkin's.

As I look through the gate, I can't see
Wilkins. But then . . .

. . . he appears (looking totally calm).
He's just sniffing a piece of burrito
that someone's dropped by his gate.

Then he turns. He sees me in the bin, and
he thinks I'm trapped. He gives me a look,
as if to say: *Don't worry, Rory, I am coming
FOR YOU!* And then he LAUNCHES
himself at the gate.

Cat pushes the bin towards him, I bend down, Wilkins and I *hug* and for about six seconds I'm *totally happy.*

But then *my mum appears* from Mrs Welkin's house. She sees me.

She also sees that I am not lying in
bed doing homework, but am, in fact,
charging up and down the street in a bin.

To describe how Mum *reacts* I will first have to tell you about the *Orient*, which was Napoleon's biggest ship ...

One night a flaming cannonball hit its gunpowder store, and it EXPLODED in a *blast* that *shook the sky* right across Egypt.

That is the kind of blast that happens right now.

'RORY,' Mum screams, 'GET HOME NOWWWW!!!'

As I look up at her, I'm thinking I could cry, and I don't want to in front of Cassidy. I also don't want to run home just because Mum is *shouting in the street*.

I turn to Mrs Welkin, who is behind
Mum, and I say, 'Mrs Welkin, I've been
getting *lonely* at home . . . could I borrow
Wilkins for company?'

She gives me a wise, kind look.

'I'm sure Wilkins would *love* to visit
you, Rory,' she says.

She lifts him
into the bin. She
also gives me
his favourite
squeaky
hedgehog.

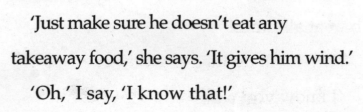

'Just make sure he doesn't eat any
takeaway food,' she says. 'It gives him wind.'

'Oh,' I say, 'I know that!'

I definitely DO know that. Wilkins eats the food that people drop, and then he does LETHAL FARTS. He does one now. (I can feel it echoing around the bin.)

'But the main thing is,' says Mrs Welkin, 'with this dog thief about you must watch him at all times!'

'Oh, I will do that!' I promise.

'I know you will,' says Mrs Welkin.

And with that we head off towards
home. I don't even mind any more about
Mum shouting. We have Wilkins, and
nothing else matters.

As we cross the street we pass Dale and
Shaza, who just moved into the flat at the
bottom of our garden. They're all right.
But they have a huge lethal *Rottweiler*
called Bizmo.

Bizmo thinks it's WEIRD I'm in the bin.

He starts to bark. *RUR-RUR-RUR*,
he goes, in a deep, bear-like growl, as
if he's saying, '*I cannot allow THIS on
my street!*'

Wilkins sticks his face over the bin. *RRRR – RRRR – RRRR*, he goes, as if to say, '*This is NOT your street. It belongs to ME, and RORY, and MRS WELKIN!*'

And the trouble is . . . as he does that,
he knocks out his hedgehog.

RIGHT! thinks Bizmo (the big greedy
bully), *I will have THAT!* And he picks up
the hedgehog, and walks off with it.

Wilkins is *furious*. He barks, *rur-rur-rur*
– as if to say: *You have taken my hedgehog,
and I will TAKE YOU DOWN, Bizmo.
I will TAKE YOU DOWN!*

Dale and Shaza walk off. Wilkins runs
up my chest, leaps and then SOARS
INTO THE SKY like he's SUPERDOG . . .

He is *flying* down towards Bizmo –
teeth ready to bite, BUT unfortunately *as
he does* . . .

Brendan O'Gooley is crossing the street past Bizmo. Brendan is the biggest, toughest *knucklehead* around. He *catches* Wilkins and squeezes him in his meaty hands.

'*Don't you touch our dog!*' I shout.

'You stop your dog barking,' he says,
'or *I* will!'

And he *dunks* Wilkins into the bin.

'*I don't want to hear another dog barking
EVER AGAIN!*' he growls.

Brendan strides off up the street.

And, staring after him, I say to the Cat, 'Did you hear him? He said he didn't want to hear *any* dogs *ever again*. He practically ADMITTED he's taking the dogs, and I say he's an evil, ignorant scumbag, and I say we *BRING HIM DOWN*!!'

She gives me one of her most catty looks.

'Don't you think you're being a bit *prejudiced*?' she says.

I say, 'HUH!'

CHAPTER THREE:
A Quick Word about Prejudice

Our head teacher, Ms Birkinstead, is always giving assemblies about prejudice, which is when you judge someone on how they look, which, she says, is very, very bad.

'You don't judge a book by its cover,'

she says.

Which I always think is RUBBISH.

I *always* judge a book by its cover –
e.g. if it is called *Fun with Tractors*, and it
has a picture of a *tractor* . . .

. . . I don't read it.

Or, if the book is called *Ten Little Unicorns*,
or *Ten Little ANYTHING*, I *definitely* don't
read it, because in those books the SAME
THING always happens.

First there are ten little unicorns
trotting out to play (clip-clop, clip-clop).

But then one trots away.

Then there are nine little unicorns
trotting out to play (clip-clop, clip-clop).

But then another trots away.

Then there are eight little unicorns
trotting out to play (clip-clop, clip-clop).

And by the time there are *seven* little
unicorns (trotting out to play) you are
wishing you could . . .

. . . crush all the unicorns with a big hammer.

You want all unicorns to trot *down a toilet,* and you want them to be FLUSHED out over a swamp.

SPLASH!

All right, *OK* . . . I know you should not
judge everyone just on their face.

SWAMP

But the reason I am judging Brendan O'Gooley is because he has just *shoved his face* into mine, and then he said, 'I don't want to hear another dog barking ever again!' Plus he has blond greasy hair in a centre parting, so his head looks like a BUM.

'I am not saying for DEFINITE that Brendan is a bad guy, who is stealing all the dogs,' I say

to Cat. 'But I am *definitely* saying he looks like a big BUMHEAD, and I *suspect* him.'

'Fair enough,' she says. 'But you'd better get EVIDENCE before you accuse him.'

She now pushes me into my house. I climb out of the bin.

'I can see his flat from my window,'
I tell her. 'I'll watch it!'

'You do that!' she says.

'Don't you want to spy on him with
me?' I ask.

'I don't think your mum is that keen on
me just now,' she says. 'So I'd better go
home.'

And she does.

Wilkins goes too. He doesn't even bother going to the living room to pull the blind. He just *shoots* up the stairs.

By the time I get into the room he's already in position.

He is looking out, like the captain of an old-style ship staring at the horizon.

'Captain Wilkins,' I say, 'do you mind if I join you?'

He shuffles over to make room. He then looks out of the window. *I* look out of the window.

And THAT is how the Great Stakeout starts.

CHAPTER FOUR:
The Great Stakeout

By the way, *the Great Stakeout* is NOT
a great juicy steak that gets left out.
A stakeout is when detectives look out,
to gather EVIDENCE.

The first thing that happens – at 12.52 hours – is we see Mrs Crompton's cats come into *our* garden. They scratch their claws on our treehouse tree. Wilkins goes *rrrrrr*.

Then I look into the bathroom window of my arch enemy Michael Beard, who lives three doors down. He is dancing around in his underpants looking like an eejit. I laugh. That's at 12.54 hours.

Then at 13.06 hours, I see Dale and Shaza coming back. He is holding a black coat. I remember the dog thief had a black coat. *Interesting*, I'm thinking. *Very, very interesting.*

Then I see Brendan 'the Bumhead'
O'Gooley leaving the house. He is quite
literally HOLDING A DOG CAGE!!
*He is so obviously the
thief!* Why does
no one STOP him?

Then we see nothing for quite a
while. (And that includes my so-called
Accomplice, Cassidy. I'm thinking: *Where
the HECK is she?*)

Then – at 14.06 hours – she
comes out of her house.
She jumps up on her wall,
and she just stands there,
looking like a tightrope
walker.

And about one second after that, Rupert Beard (Michael Beard's even more annoying brother) goes by. The Beards both want to be jockeys. They're both tiny, and they're such *show-offs*. Rupert Beard is on his bike – making it rear up like a horse and he's fully dressed – *head to foot* – in brand-new jockey clothes.

'Hey, Catty-Cat Callaghan!' he calls.
'Do you like my new bike?'

'Yes,' says Cassidy. 'And I like your hat!'

'Have it!' he says, and Frisbees it *at her*.

So now *cannonballs* are booming in my head. I'm thinking: *How come he's got so much money that he's got a new bike and he's giving out hats?* I'm thinking: *Cat Callaghan is MY name for her!* (*How come HE's using it?*)

But then, as Rupert Beard swoops round the corner into Jay Byrne Road (still on one wheel), someone is coming the other way, and it is ...

Mrs Matringham, the 'Dog Lady'.

She is an *enormous* lady, who has a pack of SIX dogs. She LOVES them. She calls them all after celebrities.

Her last two are *Nicki Minaj* and *Ed Sheeran* (her two short-haired Yorkshire terriers).

Ed Sheeran is a little ginger dog. He's got beady eyes. He can see a cat across the street, and he *charges out*.

Rupert Beard has to swerve.

But prime suspect Brendan O'Gooley is just arriving in his van and Beard *smacks into the side*.

Brendan slams on his brakes, and leaps out. Everyone SCARPERS. I can't believe it. He clears the street in one second.

'I don't know what YOU'RE looking at!' he screams, suddenly turning to *me*.

TERRIFIED, I shut the window so fast

I bop Wilkins on his nose. He does a fart

that smells of garlic, then falls to the floor.

I've shut the window just in time.

Two seconds later, Mum comes in.

'Rory Branagan,' she says, 'what *are* you doing?'

I play it cool. 'Oh,' I say, 'I've just been reading about Napoleon.'

I pat the book, as if we're old friends.

'Have you?' says Mum.

'Yes,' I tell her. 'Cover to cover.'

Mum shows me a page for about 0.4 seconds.

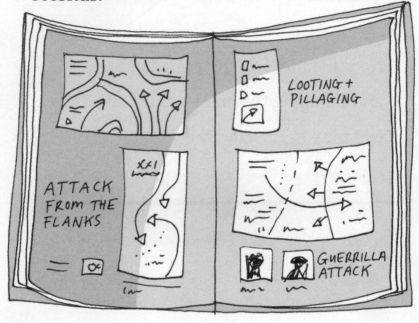

'So what was that bit about?' she asks.

'It's about Napoleon's tactics in battle,' I tell her.

'Go on then,' she says. 'Tell me about his tactics in battle.'

'Well,' I say (and I'm trying to remember), 'there is Attack from the Flanks (when Napoleon would attack from the flanks). And there is Looting and Pillaging (when he would take the enemies' stuff). And there's Guerrilla Attacks, which is when he would send in gorillas (because sometimes he'd come to a big castle, and soldiers couldn't get in, but gorillas could, or even monkeys) . . .'

'Send in the **monkeys!**'

'RORY!' shouts Mum. 'It's "Guerrilla Attack", not "Gorilla Attack". That is where troops *hide* and then they leap out and *fight*, and then they *hide* again. Don't just make things up: you need to *understand*! Your imagination will get you into a lot of trouble one of these days!'

With that, she pulls the curtains SHUT.

'And if I find out you've been staring out of that window any more,' she says, 'it'll be boarded up.'

CHAPTER FIVE:
Paperwork

After that my mum's lurking about.

I'd better not look out of that window to do any detectiving, I think. So I decide to do all my paperwork.

I think this could actually be my favourite thing about being a detective: I get out all my pens and rulers, and I draw a map of my area, marking up all the places of IMPORTANCE to the CRIME.

And when I have done that I draw a diagram of the *five* suspects' houses, and I write their names . . .

① Bumhead
② Bizmo
③ Old Lady
④ Dog Lady
⑤ Beards

After that I write up any *evidence* I've found.

Brendan O'Gooley (PRIME SUSPECT / THE BIG BUMHEAD) lives in the house on the corner in the downstairs flat.

The top flat is 'TO LET'. I know this because there is a sign outside, which Corner Boy has changed so that it says . . .

In the house next door the top flat is 'FOR SALE'. I know this because there is a sign, which Corner Boy has changed so it reads . . .

Underneath that are Dale, Shaza and Bizmo. I realise they also have a van – like Brendan (useful for transporting stolen dogs).

But I realise that it would be almost impossible for them to be handling the dogs with Bizmo around, because he'd be trying to fight them, and I *conclude* that for that reason . . .

. . . THEY ARE NOT LIKELY TO BE THE THIEVES.

Next door there is just Mrs Crompton. She owns the whole house. I think she also is very, very unlikely to be stealing dogs. She's 102, and she lives with four cats.

VERY, VERY UNLIKELY TO BE THE THIEF.

Next door to her is the Dog Lady.

POSSIBLE MOTIVE: SHE WANTS TO OWN
ALL THE DOGS IN THE WORLD.

Next to her is the house of Michael Beard, Rupert Beard and Mrs Beard (their mum). I am thinking, *I can easily imagine they* might *be taking dogs*. But I cannot think WHY.

Then someone comes in.

It's Corner Boy holding a plate of food.

'I've made some biscuits,' he says.

(They look *disgusting*. I swear he's put *maggots* in them!) 'I'm raising money for my dad, because he's still in hospital.'

'Oh, right!' I say, and I buy all of them.

I tell Corner Boy I think Brendan O'Gooley is the dog thief.

'He's probably selling them,' says Corner Boy. 'Rich people buy them. They stuff them and put them on the wall, and they make wallets out of their ears, and they have the tails sticking out of the walls for when they want to turn on the lights.'

I am trying to picture that.

'I can't believe that!' I say.

'It's true,' he replies. 'My mum read it in the paper.'

Then he goes.

But wait one moment, I think as he clumps down the stairs. *If someone is stealing dogs for money, then I bet it's the Beards. They've definitely got loads of cash all of a sudden.*

I decide I have to spy on them again. That's at 17.43 hours.

I peek out of the curtains and see the Beards are in their garden. *What are they doing?* They disappear.

I keep looking, but I don't notice anything till 18.42 hours when I see Dale and Shaza taking Bizmo out.

Moments later, Dale and Shaza are getting into their van, and I THINK I SEE Brendan. His evil face appears at the window by his door for one second. Then he goes.

But I couldn't be quite sure. It's not easy running a two-man stakeout when one of you has badly sprained his leg, and the other is a dog. Wilkins is sleeping. Sprawled on his back, he is snoring like a pirate.

I decide to join him for a moment.

But then I wake a few minutes later to find *the Cat is in my room*. She is sitting on the floor playing with Wilkins.

She's making him walk on his back legs.

He looks like a little old man (with a
very long nose). On each step he farts.
Blll–bllll–blll.

'This is *hilarious*!' she says. 'I've got
to take him outside to show this to
everyone!'

So now I'm thinking: *You've just got here. Why would you go straight out again?*

I say, 'I don't think you should take him, actually, because Mrs Welkin says I am looking after him.'

But Cassidy must know Mrs Welkin is
in the house.

She shouts . . .

'Mrs Welkin, can I take Wilkins
outside for a few minutes so he can show
off his tricks to my friends?'

I can't *believe* that. As I look at her the cannonballs are *booming* in my head. I'm thinking ...

I said she can't take him ...! How DARE she ask Mrs Welkin?

I'm thinking . . .

I'm thinking . . .

I'm thinking . . . *Bring those jockeys to me.*

I shall FLING them into space!!

But Mrs Welkin is probably just thinking that Captain Wilkins has been in my room all afternoon; he must need a poo.

She's not wrong. Captain Wilkins is now so full of wind he could blast off into space with just his own fart.

'You can only have Wilkins for FIVE MINUTES,' I tell Cat. 'Clean up after him with a plastic bag. And don't take your eye off him *for even one second.*'

She then gives me a *don't-be-an-eejit*
look, as if *I* were the one who's maybe
about to make a very bad mistake.

'I won't!' she says, and she goes.

I don't like this one bit. But there's
nothing I can do. So I just read about
Napoleon.

CHAPTER SIX:
Betrayal

In this chapter, the British catch Napoleon and say he can't be emperor any more.

They make Louis king of France instead, and banish Napoleon to a small island called Elba.

Napoleon is *furious*. He wants to
complain. Then he gets a better idea.

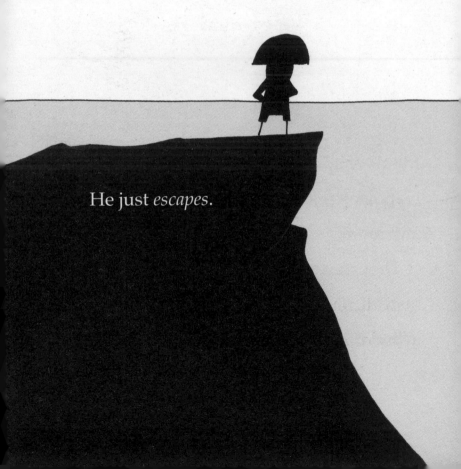

He just *escapes*.

Napoleon gets in a boat, and he sails to France.

BUT THEN ... King Louis sends a huge army of French soldiers to stop Napoleon.

And Napoleon just gets off his horse.

And he pulls off his hat, and he says:

'Here I am, kill me if you wish!'

But then the huge army of French soldiers all shout *'Long live the emperor!'* and then they ALL march back to Paris with Napoleon in charge – *doom-der-dum, doom-der-dummmm.*

I AM LOVING THIS! I am wanting to *march* out of my room, and I am wanting to hold down my brother, so I can pull out his four disgusting hairs.

(But I don't! Give me credit! I don't!)

And then, *fifty-four minutes* after leaving my room, the Cat comes back. And this is how I know I am a detective . . .

I am listening as she comes in the front door, and just by her *sound* I SUSPECT something BAD has happened. She comes slowly up the stairs.

Then I just see her pale face coming round the door, and immediately I KNOW something TERRIBLE has happened.

'Have you got Wilkins?' she says.

Oh God, this is what I feared. Right away it's like my heart's dropped down a deep, deep well.

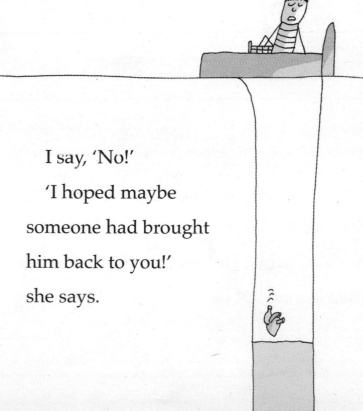

I say, 'No!'

'I hoped maybe someone had brought him back to you!' she says.

I say, 'No!' I feel so weak and dizzy, it's as if the whole world's gone white.

'I just left him outside the shop for *ten seconds* with Michael and Rupert Beard,' she says, 'while I bought a lolly. And when I came out he was gone.'

Then for a moment I'm thinking:

Wilkins has been stolen. I could cry, but I do

not want to cry.

Then I am hit by a volcano blast of hot fury.

'How do you KNOW,' I growl, 'that Rupert Beard didn't take him?'

'He came in the shop to buy Frazzles.'

'Then maybe Michael Beard got him!' I say.

'I don't think that's likely!' she replies.

'You know *nothing* about the Beards!' I say. 'They are *evil* and *greedy* and Wilkins is *valuable*! They could be about to sell him. We need to stop them FAST!'

'Look,' she says, 'we don't know anything about the Beards. We don't know ANYTHING about any of the suspects who might have taken him.'

'Oh, but we *do*!' I say.

'What do you mean?' she says.

'Because while *some* people have been outside, making friends and losing dogs,' I say, 'others have been getting EVIDENCE.'

And I just slam down the five-house diagram.

I can tell she's impressed.

I can tell she is also *curious*. She's been trying to keep away from detectiving because of my mum. But now I see she wants to help me *crack the case*.

'Mr Detective,' she says. 'Good work!'

And so now I am still very worried and angry because Wilkins is lost. But I can't help but feel a little happy, because . . .

. . . *the Great Crime-fighting Duo are BACK TOGETHER!*

CHAPTER SEVEN:
The Cat's on the Case

'Well,' she says, 'you can cross off a couple of the suspects *right away*.'

'Who?' I say.

'The old woman,' she says.

'Agreed,' I say.

'And also the Dog Lady,' she says. 'I saw her earlier. She'd just lost her two Yorkshire terriers!'

'Nicki Minaj and Ed Sheeran?!'

'*Exactly!*' says Cat. 'She was crying.'

'I am 99 per cent sure that it's Brendan. I saw him out there with a cage. I say we call the police.'

And suddenly Cat wheels round.

'I'm telling you, Rory,' she says. '*DON'T* be talking to the police!'

'*WHY?*'

'We are detectives. We don't *need* them. They'll just ask loads of questions and not DO anything, and we need to hurry. I'll sort it out myself.'

Is this true?

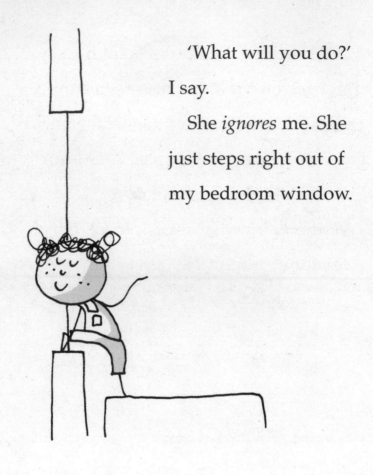

'What will you do?'
I say.

She *ignores* me. She
just steps right out of
my bedroom window.

Ten seconds later, she is standing on the
little porch outside my window, checking
out the suspects' houses.

'I'll check on the Beards first,' she says. 'I'll check on the old lady and the empty flats too. Then I'll go to Brendan's van. I can see his window's open. And I can look at Dale and Shaza's too.'

'*They* went out an hour ago!' I tell her.

'Did they?' she says.

She looks outside. 'And *they* left their bathroom window open,' she says, smiling.

'What will you do?' I say, horrified.

'Well, it was me who lost Wilkins,' she says. 'I could just go in, so quick, and check he's not there!'

I am thinking: *I definitely DON'T think you should be climbing in people's windows.* But then I think: *Wilkins could be waiting at that one, hoping someone will come.*

I say nothing.

I just watch, astonished, as the Cat
heads out to investigate.

She does not hang about.

She stretches down to the wall.

She leaps to the floor.

She springs into the tree.

On the trampoline. *Boing*.

Eight seconds later I cannot believe it –
she is just walking along the wall.

I watch as she moves swiftly along
to the Beards' back garden. She drops
silently down. She flits like a shadow into
their alleyway.

Ten seconds later . . .

I can see her inside the Beards' house.

I can see the Beards.

They look *terrifying*. Suddenly I
feel SURE they COULD be the actual
criminals! They're *definitely* evil!

I've only been round there once, when I was in kindergarten. Michael Beard *locked me in his cellar,* and said I was his *prisoner.*

I see it . . . *That's where the dogs will be right now!*

I'm thinking: *That's where the Cat will be!*

I'm thinking: *They'll be tying her up now, beside four crates of dogs that they're holding, ready to sell, so they can get cash for bikes and stupid jockey gear ...*

But then I see the Cat is *not* at the Beards, at all.

I see her
appearing in
the alleyway by
Dale and Shaza's
house.

She knocks on
their door.

Normally
when someone
knocks Bizmo
barks so loudly
the whole street
can hear. Now
their house is
silent. I can tell
they're out.

Even so, I watch – *horrified* – as Cat leaps up, sticks her head through the window, then posts herself through.

She disappears.

After that

it's a bit like

when you see

a duck dive

underwater,

and it seems to

disappear for

far too long, and

you're worrying if

the duck can breathe, or

if it's been *torn to pieces* by

an eel.

It's like that, but about ten times worse.

Then suddenly Cat *reappears* through their front door . . .

. . . and I realise I've been holding my breath. I am so dizzy with relief I just flop back on my bed.

About sixteen seconds later, she climbs
through my window. I can't believe it.
She's hardly out of breath.

I look at her a moment.

She looks at me. She looks like the cattiest Accomplice in the world.

'How did you even get into the Beards'?' I ask.

'I just told them I was looking for the dog thief,' she replies.

'Were they interested?'

'Of course,' she says. 'They've lost Steve, their greyhound.'

'*Have they?*' I ask. 'So I'd say that writes them off!'

'I'd say it does,' she replies. 'Mrs Beard was bawling. So was Michael.'

'Then I went to Dale and Shaza's,' says Cat.

'I know,' I say. 'I saw. I could not believe my eyes. Were you scared?'

'A bit,' she admits.

'What happened?'

Cat shrugs. 'I checked the bedroom, the bathroom and the kitchen,' she says, 'but I couldn't find anything odd.'

'What about the *cellar*?' I ask.

She says: '*What*? Where *is* that?'

I see I'm going to have to draw her a map.

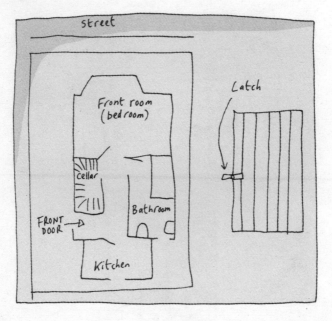

'That's where the cellar is,' I tell her, while drawing a big arrow. I also draw a picture of the kind of latch that covers its door.

'Oh my God,' she says. 'I did see a door like that!'

'Well, *that's* where the dogs would be!'
I tell her.

'Why?' says Cat.

'Because of the barking! I can't *believe* you
didn't check it! I think you need to go
again!'

The Cat says nothing.

She just heads off once again out of the window.

Off the wall.

To the ground.

Into the tree.

Trampoline.

And ten seconds later I am holding my breath once again, while she is climbing back inside.

And using my detective imagination, which – *excuse me, Mum, DOES actually think of other people!* – I am *imagining* her as she . . .

. . . climbs down on to the sink (trying not to step on the soap).

I can clearly imagine her sneaking
down the corridor.

She finds the cellar door with the latch.

I see her creeping down those dark steps, and I am thinking: *But* WHAT *is she seeing at the bottom?*

Then nothing happens. It's like when you're watching the duck that has been underwater far too long, and now you just KNOW a BIG UNDERWATER FIGHT is going on.

Meanwhile, I am staring at Dale and Shaza's flat, and I am thinking: *Please, please, please, please, please do NOT come back right now!*

And I am just thinking that WHEN . . .

Dale and Bizmo come back!!!

Dale and Bizmo go into the flat. I don't hear any sounds.

Then ...

Dale appears in the kitchen. He puts on *Pointless Celebrities*. Through the window I can see the friendly face of Alexander Armstrong. But then Dale shuts the curtains.

But they're still open a crack. I can still just see the TV. I am *guessing* that this means that Dale has NOT found the Cat.

But who knows ? The Cat is so incredibly brilliant at talking her way out of things. For all I know she could be sitting on the sofa right now with Dale and Bizmo.

But I think it's unlikely.

And then I see what is far, far more
likely to have happened . . . *When Dale
came home he found the
cellar door open
and closed it.*

Oh my God, I'm thinking, *this is
the* worst *thing that has ever happened!
Cat's trapped in their flat!*

I am desperate. I am also TERRIFIED.

And it's just then that my door opens,
and a HUGE DARK SHAPE appears.

I scream.

CHAPTER EIGHT:
A Huge Dark Shape

Then Mum turns on my light.

'Rory,' she says, 'Detective Maysmith has kindly dropped by to check you're OK.'

The big man smiles. He waves some
custard creams at me.

I haven't actually seen the police detective since the night Cat and I took down the poisoners.

'Are you OK?' he says.

He means my leg.

'I'm fine,' I tell him. 'I just have my leg in this surgical boot.'

He says nothing. I'm thinking: *Shall I tell him about Cat? She did say NEVER to speak to the police!*

I'm thinking: *But that was before she was trapped.*

'Mr Maysmith,' I say, 'you need to go to that flat down there right now!'

'Why?' he says.

'Because that's where the dog thieves are!'

Stephen Maysmith gives me a very serious look.

'What evidence do you have for that statement?' he asks.

'Earlier,' I say, 'I saw a long low dog being led off by a suspicious individual in black.'

'Did you see the person's face?' says Maysmith.

'No,' I tell him.

I can tell I have not convinced him to go to Dale's flat.

So I tell him a lie. 'But then about a minute later I saw them taking the dog into that flat.' I point clearly to Dale and Shaza's.

'Are you a hundred per cent sure the dogs are in that flat?' he asks.

'No,' I want to tell him. '*I am 99 per cent sure the dogs are in the flat of Brendan O'Gooley, but . . . right now I NEED you to go to Dale's, so you can get Cat!*'

But I don't say any of that.

And anyway he's not looking at me.

He starts checking his phone.

'I don't think there's anyone with a
criminal record in that flat,' he says.

But that's the trouble with grown-ups. They are always looking down into their phones, as if their phones lead to a library as big as a palace that contains all information . . .

But meanwhile Maysmith doesn't
actually look out of the window. I do.
And . . .

I now see Shaza coming back.

And that means she *could* be going to the cellar right now, and she *could* be about to find the Cat, who will end up stuffed on a wall.

'Mr Maysmith,' I say, 'please go there right *now*. And call in at Brendan's next door. I think he's helping them. I saw him with a dog cage.'

The police detective just stares at me.

'Oh, Rory, Rory,' he says, smiling
fondly. 'The days have *long* passed since
police officers could go busting into
houses based on the obscure tip-off of
a young boy ... These days we need
warrants, forms, *evidence.*'

I can't believe it. I see he's not going to
go. So then I do what they tell you to do
at school ...

I tell the truth.

'Wilkins has been taken (Mrs Welkin's dog),' I tell him. 'And I think that Cassidy has gone to Dale's flat to find him . . .'

(I do say: 'I *think* Cassidy has gone over there . . .' So I still might not get in trouble for sending her.)

'Well,' says Maysmith, 'I certainly HOPE she has not. Because that would be a very SERIOUS offence.'

He doesn't seem to have taken in that Cat's *in* that flat. I can't think how to make him go. I think I might cry.

'Oh, Rory,' he says fondly.

And just from his face I can see that he's about to tell me some long, boring story, and I think, if he does, my head will explode like a bomb.

But it just shows how actually you should *never* judge a book by its cover. Because then Stephen Maysmith tells me the most interesting thing anyone's ever said.

CHAPTER NINE:
Someone Actually
Tells Me Something

'I always feel protective towards you,' says Maysmith. 'Because it was me who actually found you on that day.'

'What?'

'On the day your dad ran off,' says

Maysmith, 'and you were left alone in the car . . . remember? It was *me* who found you.'

I just say, 'My dad . . . left me alone . . . in a car?'

And as I look into Maysmith's eyes I am realising he is talking about a very important memory that I had completely forgotten. But I now remember it . . .

I am seeing me and Dad in a car.

Then Dad runs off. *But where did he go?*

As I stare at Maysmith's eyes now I'm thinking: *I cannot believe it*. For the first time I've realised there was a WITNESS on the day when Dad ran off . . .

And it was me.

As Maysmith looks back at me HE is realising he has said something that he should NOT have.

'Does your mum not talk about this?' he asks.

'No!' I tell him. 'She definitely does *not*!'

He looks fierce uneasy. 'Well, probably best not to mention this,' he says.

'Anyway, I'm glad to see you're on the mend,' he continues, coughing and passing over the custard creams. 'I'd better get on!'

And he goes.

Moments later, I am looking at my open bedroom door, and I am thinking: *What did he just tell me?*

And one second later I am thinking: *And if Maysmith won't get Cat, WHO WILL?* I'm thinking: *Who could I tell?*

I'm thinking: *I could tell Mum. But she would KILL me.*

I'm thinking: *I can't tell my brother. That would be like telling Mum.*

I could tell Mrs Welkin, I think.

But then I think that if Mrs Welkin went to Dale's, there might be a big FIGHT . . .

I could tell Mrs Welkin, I'm thinking.

But then I think that, if she went to Dale's door, there might be a big FIGHT to get Cat out of that cellar and past Bizmo. And I'm thinking: *Mrs Welkin is great if you want someone to make you tea.*

But I'd say she'd not be much good in a fight.

If ONLY my dad was here, I'm thinking.
I could tell HIM.

He'd bang on Dale's door. He'd karate-chop
Bizmo...

Two seconds later, he and Cat would
be walking home along the wall being cool...

But Dad's not here.

I think it all through, like Napoleon. But the more I think, the more I can only see one possible plan, and I don't like it all . . .

I must send myself into battle.

And I can see *so* many problems with this plan. They start hitting me like cannonballs . . .

I'm thinking . . .

How will I get Dale to open the door?

Corner Boy's cookies!! I'll pretend to be selling them. He'll open up!

But they're DISGUSTING!

Doesn't matter! They took our hedgehog. They DESERVE to eat maggots!

Arming myself with cookies, I head off to war.

But there are still SO many problems, and the next is my *badly* sprained leg. Just leaving the room I clunk my surgical boot in the doorway. It lets loose an EXPLOSION OF PAIN!

But I'm not scared of a little pain. I keep going.

As I reach the bottom of the stairs I can see Mrs Welkin through the living-room door. 'Rory,' she calls, '*Country Wide* is about to start!' (She knows I LOVE *Country Wide*, because I love watching the badgers and the voles!)

I'm thinking I'd love to be on the sofa watching TV with Mrs Welkin. But I don't think Napoleon would stop, even for voles. I keep going.

As I go through the kitchen the biggest problem is going BOOM in my head . . . *BIZMO.*

Even if I can open the cellar door, how will Cat get out without being *KILLED* by the HUGE LETHAL ROTTWEILER?

And I can't think of a solution to that one.

But as I head through the garden
I think of something I learned from
Napoleon . . .

There's a time to make plans.
There's a time to STOP making plans.
There's a time for ACTION.

I figure that time
is now. And I set off
into battle. But I go in
by a way Napoleon
would never have
gone . . .

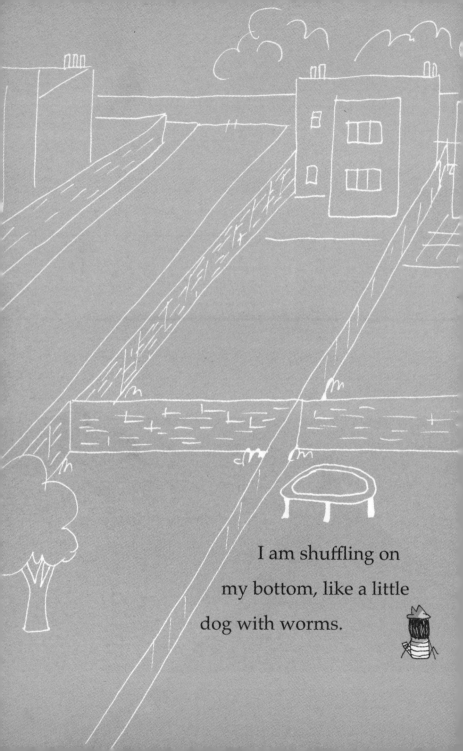

I am shuffling on
my bottom, like a little
dog with worms.

As I land in Dale and Shaza's garden I find a skateboard. *Nice*, I think, and as I head towards battle on my skateboard I realise I'm actually feeling GOOD that I'm going to get my friend back.

For a moment I feel very CONFIDENT.
I pull myself up at Dale's front door and
knock.

Then someone appears in the alleyway
behind me. I yelp.

I turn and I see it's Brendan O'Gooley.

He looks pale and stubbly with mad round eyes.

'*Can you go away?*'

I want to say. '*I am not ready to DEAL with you yet. I need to rescue my Accomplice who is trapped in a cellar!*'

'What are you doing?' he says.

'I'm selling biscuits,' I tell him. 'They're for dogs!'

Suddenly his face crumples.

'Well, I'll not be needing those!' he says. 'I lost my Gordon yesterday!'

'Gordon?'

'My dog. Have you seen him?'

'What does he look like?'

'He's a very long dog,' says Brendan (trying very hard not to cry), 'with short legs.'

'Oh,' I say. 'The furry crocodile!'

221

'Do you know something?' he asks.

'I saw him being taken away,' I tell him, 'by someone in a black coat with a black hat. I was too far off to see their face.'

'Oh God!' says Brendan, and now he properly cries.

'I've been looking for him ever since he went! At one point I heard a dog had been found, and I went rushing out with his travel cage, but' – at this point Brendan's voice goes all squeaky – 'the dog that had been found was *NOT* Gordon!'

As I watch Brendan sob I am thinking: *So that's why he's been so weird! He's lost his dog, and he's been upset!* I'm thinking: *I have spent the last few hours CERTAIN that man was a criminal. I am actually a terrible*

detective!

I'm thinking: *I have got NOWHERE at*
working out who's taking these dogs!

For all I know, I'm thinking, it's my brother who's doing it, because he's jealous of their furry faces. My brother could be with all the stolen dogs right now.

But I think it's unlikely.

And then, standing in that alleyway,
I realise that, *if* the evil criminal dog-thief
is NOT Brendan, there's really only one
other person who it could be . . .
and I've just knocked on
his door.

Dale.

As I look at his
pale face through
the window I am
realising I have
actually cracked the
case.

I also realise I am in THE DEADLIEST

OF DEADLY DANGERS!!!

CHAPTER TEN:
In the Deadliest
of Deadly Dangers

Dale opens the door.

'What do you want?' he says.

'I'm selling cookies,' I say. 'I'm raising money for Mr Gilligan who is still in hospital.'

'Oh,' says Dale. 'I don't have any money!'

He's about to close the door. But then I
get another idea!

'I've been selling for ages,' I say, 'and my foot is tired.' (I show him the surgical boot.) 'Would you like to just *have* the biscuits – for your dog?'

'Oh,' he says.

He smiles. (He actually looks nicer than you'd expect.)

'That's very good of you! Bizmo?'

Suddenly Bizmo appears.

Bizmo looks HUGE and SAVAGE and SLOBBERY.

'Bizmo,' warns Dale. 'Be *nice*.'

I hold out a biscuit to Bizmo.

He comes forward. He sniffs at it.

For a moment it's like Bizmo is at a top restaurant and he is sniffing to check on ingredients . . .

And then . . .

Rrrrr-rrrr-rrrrr, and he GEROBBLES down the biscuit. (For a moment my hand is actually INSIDE his big mouth.) Then . . .

. . . he sits. He also gives me a look as if to say: *I am such a very, very, very good boy . . . Now . . . more biscuits?*

I turn to Dale. 'Should I give him all of them?'

'Er . . . fine,' he says. 'I'll just . . .'

And he heads into the flat.

So for a moment I am having a grand old time, being the sweet boy at the door giving the dog the biscuits. But all the time I am trying to think of HOW I can get into the house.

Then suddenly I get an idea.

'Can I come in,' I ask Dale, 'and use your toilet?'

'Er,' says Dale, thinking. 'All right . . . go on.'

'Thank you,' I say.

And the next moment, I can't believe it:

I am in their flat, smelling their stinky smell (a mix of beer, ashtrays and dog).

As I hobble down their hall I check the cellar door. There *is* a latch! It IS closed!

I listen out carefully. *Can I hear dogs down below?* I am not sure. *Can I hear Cat?*

I am wanting to loosen that latch as I pass, but I am SENSING that behind me Dale is watching.

He is.

'It's the door on your right,' he says.

'Thank you,' I reply.

'Who are you talking to?' asks Shaza's voice from the kitchen.

'Just a boy,' answers Dale.

Just a boy?! I am thinking. *Just a BOY??!!* Just you WAIT to SEE what I will do! Then I think: *What will I do?* I don't know myself!

For now I go in their toilet and I wee.

As I do I notice I am splattering the floor, which my mother tells me NEVER to do. *'If you splatter,'* she says, *'wipe with a tissue!'*

I am thinking: *Should I wipe with a tissue?* Then I am thinking: *Hang on, these guys have got Cat, they might have Wilkins, and they DEFINITELY took his hedgehog . . .*

So I pee on their floor – on purpose.

As I do I'm thinking: *When I come out of this bathroom Dale must NOT be watching for me!* (I need him to get bored). So I waste time. I wash my hands. I'm almost tempted to floss my teeth.

And as I leave the bathroom the delay
has worked because . . .

I can just see him through the kitchen door. He's watching TV.

I sneak, as lightly as I can across the corridor. I reach the cellar, flip the latch, open the door, then swerve inside fast (leaving the door open just a crack).

There's someone there.

It's Cat.

She's so close I can feel her warmth. Her head is only about five centimetres from mine. There's just a crack of light shining on it.

'Hello!' she mouths.

'Hello!' I mouth back. 'Is Wilkins there?'

'Rory,' she whispers. 'We have solved the case! They're *all* down there! It's sound-proofed to hide the noise. But I've heard the people talking through this door. They're definitely selling the dogs to make money.'

Just then I hear
a low, dangerous
growl.

Cat actually smiles. (She's like this! The bigger the danger, the more she smiles!)

'We have a small problem,' she says. 'What do you say we do now?'

'I think *I* might be OK,' I say. 'I just gave that dog biscuits, but you and the other dogs need to avoid him.'

'But how will we do that?' she says.

Cat is looking up at me with hope, as if I'm Napoleon about to make a plan. But the trouble is: *I have no plan.*

I think: *I should make one.* And I do.

'Get the dogs ready,' I tell her. 'Then wait here, holding the door, till you hear a big bang. Then count to twenty, and **RUN**.'

Cat smiles. 'How will I know how quickly to count?' she asks.

'You count "one unicorn",' I say. 'Then "two unicorns", "three unicorns" . . .'

She smiles. 'Thank you for coming for me!' she says.

'Oh,' I tell her, 'you are my Accomplice. If you are caught, I will come for you!'

'*Deadly Branagan*,' she says, 'you're the best.' She squeezes my hand.

So now I am just wanting to stay in this passage for ever and ever with her, but behind me Bizmo growls again.

He is now sounding even BIGGER and more vicious.

I count one unicorn, two unicorns,
three unicorns . . .

Then I push open the door.

In the hallway Bizmo sniffs me. You can
tell he thinks it's odd I'm coming from the
cellar. But he also remembers I gave him
biscuits. He doesn't bite.

I look around. No one is watching.
Thank God.

Hobbling down the hallway I look towards the kitchen door, and it's now that I see something very surprising.

It's a photo of Dale with someone I recognise – a cool good-looking man in a leather jacket. I know exactly who THAT is . . .

Dad.

Dale sees me staring.

'How do you know my dad?' I ask him.

He looks at me, amazed.

'Your dad,' he says, 'is *Padder Branagan*?'

'Yeah, but how do you know him?'
I ask again.

'*Everyone* knows your dad,' says
Dale. 'He was a two-time World Rally
champion.'

'*Was he?!!*' I say.

'Yes!' says Dale. 'But I knew him
because he drove for Daredevil Motors,
where I worked.'

As I look at Dale I am thinking:
*I actually LIKE this guy. I want to stay
chatting to him for ever.*

But then Shaza appears.

'What took you so long in that bathroom?' she says, giving me an *evil* look.

'I was just washing my hands,' I tell her. 'And flossing my teeth.'

I shouldn't have added that.

'*What?*' she says.

'It's when you put string between your teeth,' I say. 'To remove bacteria.'

'I KNOW WHAT FLOSSING IS!'
screams Shaza. 'Get out my house or I'll
knock your teeth **RIGHT OUT!**'

As I look up at her I'm seeing I've got
this crime completely wrong. *Dale is not the
leader of the criminals. Shaza is. She's got Cat,
and a whole load of dogs, in her cellar. And if I
don't watch out, I'll end up down there too.*
I hurry home.

CHAPTER ELEVEN:
Reinforcements

And less than two minutes later I am
back in my own kitchen with Mrs Welkin.
I tell her all about Dale and Shaza and
what we've found. I tell her my plan to
get Cat out.

But before we carry it out I need to give her the bad news.

'Mrs Welkin,' I tell her, 'they've got Wilkins.'

I can see her going through all the emotions I did. First she goes *still*, then she goes *faint*, then she gets the RAGE.

'Those dirty ... *FLIP-FLAPS!*' she growls. 'That's the trouble with the world today! It's *full* of hooligans and flip-flaps! *Hooligans and flip-flaps!*'

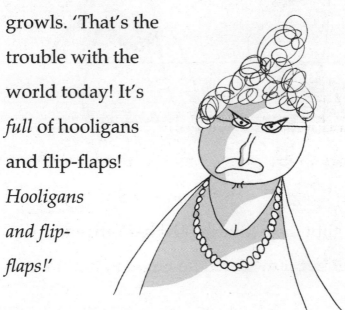

'Right,' says Mrs Welkin, already stepping out into the garden. 'I will go over there. They will give that dog *back*.'

'But they have that huge Rottweiler,' I tell her. 'I'm scared he might fight Wilkins!

'Oh,' says Mrs Welkin, 'he WILL fight Wilkins! I know flip-flap dogs like that! (The trouble is Wilkins fights them!) Wilkins thinks he's bigger than he is!'

'But maybe Wilkins will run off?' I suggest.

'But Wilkins is not fast!' says Mrs Welkin. 'He thinks he is, but he's not!'

'What will we do?'

'We need to LURE that Rottweiler out of the way!' says Mrs Welkin.

'But how will we do that?' I ask.

Mrs Welkin thinks a moment. Then her eyes light up. *She has an idea!*

'Cats!' she says. 'We'll make him chase cats!'

'But how,' I ask, 'will we make him chase cats?'

'*Tuna fish sandwiches!*' she declares.

'Do we *have* tuna fish sandwiches?' I ask.

'Oh,' says Mrs Welkin. 'We have EIGHT of them!'

'With PICCALILLI!' she roars (as if the piccalilli was the key to the whole thing).

'I shall give you the piccalilli,' she says. She hands it over, as if she's handing a mighty sword.

'And I will need a weapon of my own,' says Mrs Welkin. She nips back in the kitchen.

What weapon is she getting? I'm trying to guess. I definitely don't guess right.

Mrs Welkin comes out of the kitchen. Mrs Welkin holds up to the sky . . . a *slipper*.

'Mrs Welkin,' I say, 'are you *sure* you want to go over there with that?'

'Oh,' says Mrs Welkin. 'I may be an old girl now, but if those flip-flaps come *near* me, they will FIND OUT what I can do with a slipper.'

She slaps the slipper on her hand.

I am still worrying whether Mrs Welkin has got the right weapon, but I can see she is ready for battle.

She puts her arm round me.

We're totally together as we head off

to war.

One minute later, I'm in position (outside the flip-flaps' front door on the other side of the wall).

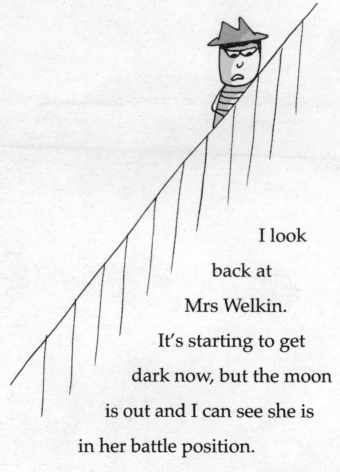

I look
back at
Mrs Welkin.
It's starting to get
dark now, but the moon
is out and I can see she is
in her battle position.

Standing on the trampoline, beside the treehouse tree, she is holding up the slipper and she's as still as a statue in the moonlight.

In front of her, on our garden wall,
she's spread out tuna fish sandwiches.
There is a cat chomping at each one.

'Are the cats ready?' I call.

'Oh,' says Mrs Welkin. 'The Cat Squad
is ready.'

'And are YOU ready?'

'I was BORN ready,' says Mrs Welkin,
and she slaps her own hand. SLAP.

I figure she's ready.

CHAPTER TWELVE:
Let Battle Commence!

I count.

One unicorn, two unicorns, three unicorns,
then . . .

I FLING the piccalilli, as hard as I can,
against the flip-flaps' window.

CRASH.

One second later, the window's gone and Dale's face is looking out of it.

I dodge down behind Brendan's wall. I'm just in time.

But behind me ... Shaza appears with Bizmo.

'Is someone there?' calls Shaza.

'Come here if you *dare*!' calls Mrs Welkin.

'Bizmo,' says Shaza, 'GET HER!'

Five seconds later, I peek over the fence.

Bizmo is chasing the cats over the wall.

'You dirty FLIP-FLAP!' roars Mrs
Welkin in a bloodcurdling scream.

Shaza looks for Mrs Welkin in the darkness.

'*You scabby old WITCH!*' she yells.

She *charges*.

But she hasn't seen the skateboard.
She treads on it, then hits the floor with
a SMACK.

Boomtown!

Boomtastic!

I want to see more of the action, but I
can't.

I dodge inside Shaza's.

As I hurry to the cellar I notice someone
has closed the latch again.

Dale sees me as I'm about to open it.

'You're too late!' I warn him. I yank open the door and release an EXPLOSION of dogs.

There's a whippet, then a greyhound,
then a big St Bernard.

Dale is PETRIFIED to see that lot.
He LEAPS through the kitchen window.

I peek into the cellar in time to see Ed Sheeran and Nicki Minaj, followed by Cat, and, bringing up the rear, like the brave dog he is ... *Captain Wilkins Welkin.*

We head down the hall to the open front door. Half the dogs have escaped. We're about to.

But now the battle turns ...

Bizmo appears.

The Dog Squad halts.

'Dogs!' I call. *'Cat! Come back!'*

Cat leads the way. She springs into the bedroom. She's followed by the terriers and Wilkins. I'm the last. I dodge through just in time.

Bizmo hits the door as I slam it shut.

BANG.

Inside the room, Cat dodges over to the window. She pulls a blind out of the way. She tries to pull open the window.

But it's stuck.

I move over to help. And at that moment Bizmo gets the door open.

He can see there're two people and three dogs in the room. He also sees those dogs are small ones that he can CRUSH.

But what he doesn't know is that one of those small dogs is Wilkins Welkin.

And as Mrs Welkin often says: Wilkins is from a long line of West Kerry dogs who are FAMOUS because they NEVER back down in a fight. And he does NOT back down now.

As Bizmo pounces. Wilkins *springs* UP.

And there's an advantage to being
small ... The small dog gets to the neck
quicker!

Wilkins bites.

Bizmo SHAKES.

Wilkins then HITS the floor.

Bizmo SPRINGS for him.

Wilkins commando-rolls from trouble.

Then he makes a Tactical Retreat under the bed.

The next bit is classic Guerrilla Warfare.

Bizmo tries to shove his big head under the bed, but he can't reach the small dogs. BOOM! Nicki Minaj *hits* from the side! (Attack from the Flanks!) She bites. She *hides*. Then . . . *BOOM!* Ed Sheeran hits from the other flank. *Sheeran bites.* Sheeran goes BERCO! Sheeran hides.

Cat grins. *The whole plan is working brilliantly!*

It's like this . . .

. . . but then the battle *turns again*, as the

enemy's fiercest fighter enters the field . . .

Shaza. She's holding the skateboard like a club. She looks at Bizmo being *wasted* by the terriers. (Ed Sheeran's gone BERSERK! He's got Bizmo by the ears and he's *shake-shake-shaking*!!)

Shaza thwacks Bizmo.

'*Get him!*' she shouts, and she points the
dog at me.

But I'm ready for him. While the Dog
Squad have been doing their Guerrilla
Warfare, I've been *Looting and Pillaging*,
and I've now got the weapon that all dogs
most fear . . .

... the **HOOVER!!!**

And as Bizmo comes for me I turn it on
and I BLAST HIM!!!

Oh my God, he LEAPS backwards!
In no time at all the enemy are in a
Full-Scale Retreat. It's like this . . .

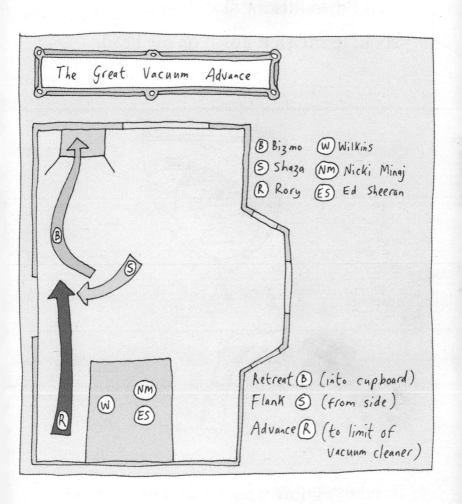

But Shaza swerves past Bizmo.

She then lifts the skateboard. She's
about to smash it down on my head.

I don't know what to do. I turn off the
Hoover for a start.

But then Captain Welkin turns.

Has he *heard* something? He has
definitely *seen* something. He has
definitely seen his *chance*. (You might even
say he's been training for this *all his life*!!)

Wilkins runs. He leaps on the bed.

He SOARS through the air.

Then he grabs the thing he saw, which

was . . .

A BLIND over the window!!!

Wilkins knows what to do with blinds. He GRABS it in his mouth, and he falls to the windowsill, going *rrrrr-rrrrr-rrrr*.

And it's one of those moments when you think there must actually be a god!

As Wilkins releases the blind I see what is almost his worst nightmare: there are *cats* on that front wall.

But behind that wall I see *reinforcements* – good ones too. I can see Corner Boy, I see Michael Beard, Rupert Beard, I can see the Dog Lady with all four remaining members of her Dog Squad.

They're looking through the window.
They're seeing me (with the Hoover) . . .
Shaza (with the skateboard) . . . Bizmo
who's trying to shake off Nicki Minaj and
Ed Sheeran who've got him by the ears.
(It looks like he's *wearing a hat* that's *made
entirely from dog*.)

'THESE ARE THE THIEVES!' I shout.
And the Beards don't need telling
twice to join a fight. Those jockeys leap,
screaming, across the front wall.

All the dogs are barking. And I am happy
to say that THIS gets the *attention* of . . .

Stephen Maysmith, the police detective.

He is round the corner taking photographs of the lamppost where the furry crocodile was stolen. He doesn't think anything of the noise at first.

Then he does.

By now the noise is *louder*. The Beards
are kicking in the front window: SMASH.
The Dog Lady, seeing her Yorkshire
terriers, is screaming, '*Oh, my poor babies*!'
And Nicki Minaj and Ed Sheeran – leaping
out of the window – are being reunited
with their owner and they're *howling*, and
I swear . . . *those dogs can SING!*

Maysmith comes running.

Inside, Shaza sees the battle's turned.

She *sprints* off down the corridor. Bizmo

follows.

I follow too. And I've chased them as far as the kitchen before I remember my *very* badly sprained leg, and I suddenly have an EXPLOSION OF PAIN . . .

. . . which feels like the Battle of Waterloo is happening inside my foot.

At that moment Stephen Maysmith enters the scene. He's charging up the corridor like a hippo behind me.

'Just WHAT is going on in here?' he is shouting.

Not much, big feller, I'm thinking. *The main fighters have left.*

I'm thinking: *I should follow.*

I hurry out.

In the garden, Dale is being pinned against the wall by Gordon and the St Bernard, and they're barking.

Bizmo is on the floor, *dazed*. And Wilkins Welkin has him by the tail, and he is *SHAKING that tail*, going *rrrr-rrrr-rrrr*, as if to say: *I said I'd take you down, and I've taken you DOWN, Bizmo. You are DOWN!*

Shaza dodges round the barking dogs.
Leaping up on to her garden wall, she
thinks she's about to run off.

She doesn't know this is the moment
Mrs Welkin has been *waiting* for.

Mrs Welkin has been waiting by the
trampoline like a flamingo by a pond.

'You dirty FLIP-FLAP!' she calls, then she leaps like a ninja across the trampoline. She bounces, then comes down with her slipper going **SLAP.** And I could not say what happens next. (I don't want to get Mrs Welkin in trouble with the police.) But over the next minute Shaza certainly FINDS OUT what Mrs Welkin can do with a slipper.

And then I turn
and see Stephen
Maysmith coming out into the
garden and I see he's about to get
the baddies. I also look over Cat's garden
wall and I see something very important.
It's *Mum* appearing in the car.

I think: *If I go NOW, I might make it back
to bed before she knows I'm gone.*

I leave the battlefield like I'm a World
Rally champion.

CHAPTER THIRTEEN:
Back at the Base

I am back in my room before Mum enters the house. I am in time to see the police arrest Dale and Shaza in the garden. As they do she looks up at me.

I think: *We took you DOWN!*

I see Cat walking along her own garden wall holding Wilkins in her arms. He's *loving* it! His head's tipped back and he's smiling.

I open my window. 'Guys,' I whisper.

They both smile up at me.

'You were EPIC!' I tell them.

'I wouldn't use that word,' says Mrs Welkin. 'I'd say we were *boomtastic*!'

'I'd just say we were *deadly*,' says Cat. 'And I was proud to be on our side.'

'I'd say the same,' I tell them. 'But would you mind not telling anyone I was there?'

'All right,' says Mrs Welkin.

'All right, Mr Detective,' says Cat. Then she smiles. Then she winks. Then she goes.

One second later, I hear my mum
coming, and I shut the window just in time.

I can see right away Mum is in a very
good mood.

'Rory,' she says, 'what have you been
doing?'

As I look back at her I think I'd *love* to tell her everything I've done, especially since it proves I *do* think of other people, and I *do* understand about Napoleon, and I *am* a real detective (who can collect evidence and plan). But I don't.

'Well,' I tell her, 'I don't want to tell you some story!'

My mum gives me a smile that's as wide as the sea.

'Are you OK?' she says.

'Oh,' I tell her, 'I'm grand!'

'I'm your mother,' she says. 'I LOVE you. That's all I ever need to know.'

Then she just LOOKS at me.

I know what that look means. I see she wants to hug me. I see there's nothing I can do about it.

I just let her. She hugs me, and I lie
back like I'm bobbing on a Lilo on the sea,
and I relax.

'You're a good boy,' she says. 'Unlike
your brother!'

His BIG
HEAD appears.

'I heard
that!' he
says. He's got
shaving foam
on his top lip so
it looks like he's
got a little white
moustache.

Mum and I both crack up.
'What?' says my brother.
'Are you *laughing* just because
I'm shaving? SO WHAT if I'm
shaving?'

My mum is shaking as she laughs, but I can tell she doesn't want my brother to see.

'I was only joking!' she calls to my brother.

'Huh!' he says.

'I'd better go and speak to him!' she whispers to me (giving me a kiss). '*Bye!*'

Next Mrs Welkin appears.

'Mrs Welkin,' I say, 'I shall never judge a book by its cover again! You sure know how to fight!'

'And you know when to ask for help!' she says. Her eyes twinkle.

'By the way,' she says, 'there's a visitor for you.'

'Who is it?' I ask (as if I didn't know!).

'He wants to know if he can come in,' she says.

'He can,' I say.

A moment later, Wilkins's long nose pokes through the door.

'Mrs Welkin,' I say, 'do you think he could stay over?'

'I think Wilkins would be *delighted* to stay over,' says Mrs Welkin. 'But you both need to sleep or I'll take him home!'

'We definitely will!' I promise.

He is looking at me with his head cocked to the side.

'Here, boy,' I say to Wilkins.

You don't command that dog twice.

Straight away Wilkins leaps. His top end soars on to my bed.

But his bottom end falls short by a good half-metre.

Wilkins scrambles up and lies down. I
do too and Mrs Welkin turns off the light.

I sniff the fur on Wilkins's head (which smells of biscuits). I also smell his fart (which smells of beans). And I think of the battle of the flip-flaps' flat. I think of Mrs Welkin with her slipper raised in the moonlight . . .

Then I think of Dad. He's driving cars in the World Rally Championship, and crowds are cheering!

Then I think of Dad leaving me in a car while he runs off. *But where did he go? I am thinking. And will I ever find him?*

But then I think: *I don't care if he's far,
far off, across deep, wide seas.*

I feel like Napoleon when they put him
on Elba. *I don't care how far I must go*, I am
thinking. *I don't care what dangers might lie
in the way.*

*I will go with my friends by my side. And
we'll find him.*

Then, knowing my friends are close by right now, I fall asleep.

341

And I dream of cars. I dream of dogs.

I dream of Dad.

The End

That weekend, we had the BIGGEST,
BEST school fete the world has ever
known!!

We had sumo wrestlers . . .

. . . a bouncy castle . . .

. . . and Corner Boy did guinea-pig racing.

We put a big stunt-man crash mat under the factory and people paid a tenner to hurl themselves off.

People were selling EVERYTHING.
One guy sold the entire contents of his
house. His sister was crying: 'Don't
sell my Barbies!' And so people started
buying the Barbies, then they gave them
back.

Corner Boy shouted, 'If you give me a tenner, I'll sing *It Ain't Me* by Selena Gomez!'

Steven McEver shouted, 'I'll give you twenty, if you DON'T!'

Corner Boy shouted, 'It's a deal!'

And fair play to Steven McEver – he paid up.

Mr Meeton held a massive line dance.
You had to wear costumes borrowed from
the drama department. Someone who
was dressed up as a stegasaurus speared

a dinner lady. Corner Boy laughed so much, he blasted Miwadi cordial down his nose. I have never seen someone laugh that hard.

My good friend Mrs Welkin came, bringing twelve cakes. I helped her sell them, and I am proud to say we sold every single slice. (Fair enough: her cakes are delicious!)

Wilkins Welkin came.

He took part in the Dog Race, and he got the special prize – a cake made from mince.

(He hadn't won. He stole it. He also cheated by starting five seconds early, but no one minded. Everyone loves Wilkins.)

People came from all over. A black
Rolls-Royce arrived. Two men got out
in top hats. They opened the door to
a powerful-looking man. He also had a
top hat.

'Watch out,' whispered Mrs Welkin.

'That's Michael Mulligan, the gangster.'

To be continued ...